TINKER BELL
STORY OF THE MOVIE

Bath · New York · Singapore · Hong Kong · Cologne · Delhi · Melbourne

On a chilly winter's night in London, a baby lay peacefully in her crib. As her mobile twirled, the baby let out her very first laugh and – as with all first laughs – a fairy was born!

The laugh floated out of the window and attached itself to a dandelion wisp. It flew above the human world straight towards the Second Star to the Right and through a burst of light into Never Land!

The laugh floated towards Pixie Hollow, a magical place in the heart of Never Land where the Never fairies live.

"Oh, my! Come on! Let's go!" the fairies cried. They followed the laugh as it made its way towards the Pixie Dust Tree.

A dust-keeper, named Terence, sprinkled some pixie dust on the laugh. It made a tinkling sound and took the shape of a fairy.

Queen Clarion approached. "Born of laughter, clothed in cheer, happiness has brought you here. Welcome to Pixie Hollow," she said. The newcomer flapped her wings. She could fly!

5

Queen Clarion waved her hand and some toadstools sprang up. Fairies began to place objects on them. Rosetta, a garden fairy, brought a flower. A water fairy named Silvermist carried a droplet of water. Iridessa, a light fairy, had a glowing flower lamp, while a fast-flying fairy named Vidia set down a whirlwind.

"These objects will help you find your talent," the queen explained.

The new fairy timidly placed her hand on the flower. Its glow instantly faded. She reached for the water droplet, but its glow faded, too. The new fairy was discouraged. But as she passed a hammer, it started to glow. Then it flew straight to her!

"I've never seen one glow that much," said Silvermist. Rosetta agreed. "Li'l daisy-top might be a very rare talent indeed!"

Vidia fumed. She had one of the strongest and rarest talents in Pixie Hollow and she wasn't looking for competition.

"Come forward, tinker fairies," called the queen, "and welcome the newest member of your talent guild – Tinker Bell!"

"Haydee hi, haydee ho! I'm Clank!" boomed a large fairy.

"We're pleased as a pile of perfectly polished pots that you're here," added Bobble, a tinker who wore dewdrop glasses.

"You have arrived at a most wondrous and glorious time!" Clank said as they flew above Pixie Hollow. "It's almost time for the changing of the seasons!"

"Welcome to Tinkers' Nook!" Bobble announced.

Tinker Bell saw a small courtyard lined with twig-and-leaf cottages. Fairies were fixing and fashioning all kinds of amazing, useful objects.

Clank and Bobble dropped Tinker Bell off at her own little house. All the clothes in her closet were much too big. Luckily, Tink knew just how to fix them.

Tinker Bell put on her new dress, tied her hair up and reported to the workshop.

Soon Fairy Mary – the no-nonsense fairy who ran Tinkers' Nook – arrived.

"So dainty!" Fairy Mary exclaimed as she looked at Tink's hands. "Don't worry, dear, we'll build up those tinker muscles in no time."

Then, after reminding Clank and Bobble to make their deliveries, Fairy Mary was gone.

A little while later, Tink, Clank and Bobble set out to deliver some springtime items to the nature fairies.

Suddenly, the fairies heard a sound behind them.

"Sprinting Thistles! Aaaaagh!" screamed Clank. The weeds nearby had come to life and were rushing towards them!

The wagon flew down the path and crashed in the middle of Springtime Square.

Thankfully, the tinkers were unhurt, and they began to make their deliveries. There were rainbow tubes for Iridessa, milkweed-pod satchels for Fawn and pussy-willow brushes for Rosetta.

Iridessa explained that she would roll up rainbows, put them in the tubes, and take them to the mainland.

"What's the mainland?" the new fairy asked.

"It's where we're going for spring, to change the seasons," replied Silvermist.

Next, the tinkers stopped at the Flower Meadow. Vidia zipped by, using her whirlwind to pull pollen from flowers.

"Hi!" said Tinker Bell. "What is your talent?"

"I am a fast-flying fairy. Fairies of every talent depend on me," answered Vidia. She made it clear that she didn't think much of tinker fairies.

Tink was insulted. "When I go to the mainland, I'll prove just how important we are!" she replied.

12

Tink flew off, grumbling to herself. Soon, however, she was distracted by something shiny down on the beach. She flew closer. It was a coin! Tink began digging, and before long she had found all sorts of treasures.

"Lost Things," said Clank, when Tink arrived back at the workshop. "They wash up on Never Land from time to time."

Fairy Mary whisked Tink's trinkets away. The Queen's Review of the springtime preparations was that night and there was still a lot to do. Tink knew this was her chance to prove just how important a tinker's talent really was!

That evening, the Minister of Spring welcomed Queen Clarion to the review ceremony. Suddenly, Tinker Bell arrived.

"I came up with some fantastic things for tinkers to use when we go to the mainland!" she called.

Before the queen could say anything, Tink pulled out a homemade paint sprayer. But instead of spraying colour, it exploded, making a huge mess!

The queen looked at Tinker Bell kindly. "Tinker fairies don't go to the mainland," she said. "All the springtime work is done by the nature fairies. I'm sorry."

Tink returned to the workshop. "Being a tinker stinks," she grumbled. "Why don't we get to go to the mainland?"

"The day you can magically make the flowers grow or capture the rays of the sun, you can go. Until then, your work is here," said Fairy Mary impatiently. Tink smiled slyly – she had an idea.

The next morning, Tink found her friends at the Pixie Dust Well. "If you could teach me your talents, maybe the queen would let me go to the mainland," Tink said.

Reluctantly, Tink's friends agreed to help. No fairy had ever changed his or her talent before!

Silvermist was first. The water fairy showed Tink how to place a dewdrop on a spiderweb. But each time Tink tried, the dewdrop burst in her hands.

Next, Iridessa demonstrated how to give fireflies their glow. She captured light in a bucket and scattered it. But when Tink tried, the light wouldn't stick to her fingers. She threw the bucket down in frustration and the light spilled in every direction.

15

Fawn had Tink's animal-fairy lesson all planned. "We're teaching baby birds how to fly," she announced.

Fawn showed Tink what to do. Unfortunately, Tink's bird was terrified. He didn't want to go anywhere. Then Tink saw a majestic bird flying overhead and decided to ask for its help. She waved her hand and tried to get the bird's attention.

The scout fairies looked to see what was going on. "Hawk! Hawk!" they yelled, sounding their warning horns.

Tink spotted a tree with a knothole and rushed straight for it, but the hole was already occupied – by Vidia. CRACK! The hawk broke through the bark with his beak. The two fairies had to get out of there – fast! They jumped down a hole into a long, dark tunnel.

When Vidia reached the end of the tunnel, she could see the hawk on a nearby branch. She stopped in the nick of time – but Tink accidentally slammed into her. Vidia went shooting out of the tree! The hawk opened his beak, ready to strike.

Fairies pelted the hawk with berries, rocks, and twigs, and luckily it flew away. But Vidia was furious, and Tink felt awful.

A little while later, Tinker Bell sat on the beach. "Great," she muttered. "At this rate, I should get to the mainland right about, oh, never!"

She angrily threw a pebble and heard a CLUNK! It was a broken porcelain music box. By the time her friends found her, Tink was busily putting her discovery back together.

"Do you even realise what you're doing?" asked Rosetta. "Fixing stuff like this – that's what tinkering is!"

"Who cares about going to the mainland anyway?" Silvermist added.

But Tink still wanted to go, so she went to see Vidia, the only fairy she thought might be able to help. Vidia had an evil idea, and suggested that Tink capture the Sprinting Thistles to prove that she would be a good garden fairy. Tink knew that Vidia's plan was her last chance to go to the mainland.

"Hi-yah! Git! Git!" Tinker Bell cried as she rode out into Needlepoint Meadow atop Cheese the mouse.

"It's working!" Tink cried joyfully. But as she headed back to the meadow, Vidia put her evil plan in to action, and quietly blew open the corral gate. The Thistles ran away towards Springtime Square, trampling over the carefully organized springtime supplies!

Everything was destroyed. And it was all Tinker Bell's fault.

"I'm sorry," Tinker Bell whispered as she took to the sky.

A little while later, Tink went to the Pixie Dust Well and told her friend Terence she was leaving Pixie Hollow. He kindly gave her a double scoop of the glittering dust.

"Thanks, Terence," said Tink.

Terence was surprised she knew his name. "I'm just a dust-keeper," he said, "not exactly seen as the most important fairy in Pixie Hollow."

"You're probably the most important one there is!" Tink argued. "Without you, no one would have any magic! You should be proud!"

"I am," Terence replied.

Tink could tell he knew she wasn't proud of her own talent.

Tink then stopped in to visit the workshop one last time. She did love to tinker – even though her contraptions never worked.

Just then, she noticed something. It was the pile of trinkets she had found on the beach.

"Lost Things...that's it!" she cried. She went to her worktable and started to tinker.

That night, Queen Clarion gathered all the fairies. She explained there wasn't time to replace what had been ruined.

"Wait!" Tinker Bell cried, landing in the middle of the square. "I know how we can fix everything!"

Tink demonstrated her paint sprayer, which she had fixed so that it worked perfectly. She had also designed other speedy machines.

Vidia was furious. "Corral the Thistles...," she muttered. "I should have told you to go after the hawk!"

Queen Clarion overheard this. She looked sharply at Vidia and told her to chase down each one of the Thistles. Vidia flew away.

The queen turned to Tink. "Are you sure you can do this?" she asked.

"I'm a tinker, and tinkers fix things," Tink replied confidently. "But I can't do it alone!"

All the fairies offered to help, and soon the square was filled with piles and piles of useful objects.

Tink showed a group of fairies how to assemble a machine to make berry paint. As soon as all the pieces of the machine were put together, the berries were crushed and dozens of buckets were filled to the brim with paint.

Next, Tink used a glove and a harmonica to make a vacuum. The fairies could use it to collect hundreds of seeds at a time.

Everywhere she looked, Tinker Bell could see baskets and buckets of springtime supplies. Her plan was working!

Early the next morning, Queen Clarion and the ministers of the seasons flew to the square. They couldn't believe their eyes – there were more springtime supplies than they had ever seen!

As the sun began to rise, the Everblossom opened, giving off a golden glow. It was time to take spring to the mainland! The fairies cheered.

"You did it, Tinker Bell!" Queen Clarion exclaimed.

"We all did it," Tink replied.

25

"Can't Tink come with us?" Silvermist asked.

"It's okay," Tink protested. "My work is here."

Fairy Mary gave a little whistle, and Clank and Bobble appeared with the music box Tink had mended.

"Actually ran across this myself many seasons ago," said Fairy Mary. "Didn't have a clue how to fix it. But you did, Tinker Bell. And I'd imagine there's someone out there who's missing this. Perhaps a certain tinker fairy has a job to do after all… on the mainland."

And so Tink flew with the other fairies towards London. When they arrived, everything was cold and the landscape was grey.

The fairies spread out across the city. A light fairy melted the frost on a tree branch. A water fairy sprinkled pixie dust on a frozen pond to thaw the ice. The animal fairies gently woke the hibernating creatures tucked inside the trees. Soon flowers bloomed and baby birds took flight.

Tink was amazed by the magic her friends created.

27

Now it was time for Tinker Bell to make her special delivery. She sprinkled some of the extra pixie dust Terence had given her on the music box, to make it fly.

As Tink passed a bedroom window, both she and the music box began to glow. Tink knew that the owner of the music box must live there. She set the box on a windowsill and peered into the room.

Tink tapped on the glass and ducked out of sight. In a few moments, a little girl named Wendy Darling poked her head out the window.

Wendy's face filled with happiness. She took a small key from a chain around her neck and turned it in a slot. The music box began to play!

The fairies' work was done. It was time for them to return to Never Land.

From then on, Tink used her rare talent to make the lives of everyone in Pixie Hollow just a little bit better. She was proud to be a tinker fairy!

THE END

30